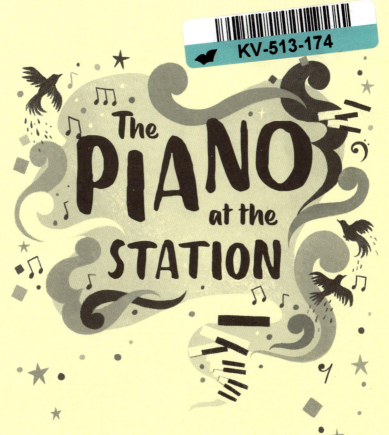

The PIANO at the STATION

HELEN RUTTER

ILLUSTRATED BY
ELISA PAGANELLI

Barrington Stoke

The
PIANO
at the
STATION

First published in 2023 in Great Britain by
Barrington Stoke Ltd
18 Walker Street, Edinburgh, EH3 7LP

www.barringtonstoke.co.uk

A CIP catalogue record for this book is available
from the British Library upon request

ISBN: 978-1-80090-218-3

Printed in Great Britain by Charlesworth Press

CHAPTER 1

"LACEY LAYTON!" Mr Jenson yells. "I am sick and tired of hearing your voice."

I'm about to get kicked out – again. I just need to say one more thing and I'll be free.

I hate Maths more than any other subject. Well, actually it's Mr Jenson I hate more than any other teacher. I used to be pretty good at Maths in primary school.

I consider keeping my mouth shut for a second. Maybe I'll stay and mess with Mr Jenson for a bit longer, but then he gives me a look. It's a look that says he's disgusted by me and would rather be teaching anyone else in the whole world. That does it – I can't keep it in.

"Well, I'm sick and tired of hearing your voice, sir," I say with a smirk. It works.

"Out!" he shouts.

None of the teachers seem to understand that I don't care. I don't want to be in their boring lessons, so it's hardly a punishment to get kicked out, is it? Anyway, I only said what Mr Jenson said to me. Why do I get kicked out and he's still free to teach his boring class?

So I'm soon sitting in ISO (isolation) yet again. The headteacher, Mrs Hukin, spots me from her office and shakes her head.

"What are we going to do with you, Lacey? That big brain of yours is being wasted. You spend more time here than in the classroom."

"I love it here, miss," I reply.

"Mmm, I'm sure you do," says Mrs Hukin. "We might need to chat to your mum again, see what we can do to make school a bit easier for you."

"Mum's busy, miss. She won't answer the phone today." This is a lie. Mum's shift will have finished by now. She'll be in the kitchen drinking tea with Auntie Jackie before her next shift starts.

"Well, you are on your last chance, Lacey," Mrs Hukin goes on. "Try to stay out of trouble for a while, hey? What are you doing at lunch-time? I know you find break-times complicated."

"It's not me, miss," I say. "Everyone starts on me for no reason."

"Well, stay out of it today, OK? Find something else to do or somewhere else to be."

"Yes, miss."

I don't want the school to call Mum again. It's not that she's bothered about me getting in trouble. I think she actually finds it pretty funny. Mum says I remind her of her when she was young. But I don't want to have to deal with the other kids making comments about her. Seeing the way she is and saying that's why I'm like I am.

The last time Mum was in, she'd been singing down the halls, looking in all her old classrooms and pulling faces at the teachers. Then Alyssa Harris made some snooty comment about how rough Mum was. You can't let someone comment on your mum and not do something about it. I had to punch Alyssa in the face, didn't I?

I hate Alyssa and her posh mates. They think they are better than me.

*

At lunch, I try to keep my head down like Mrs Hukin said. Mum's already had two calls from Teresa and Britt's school this week, so she doesn't need another call about me. Teresa secretly put her teacher on her Insta live again. She films everything – it's like she's addicted.

Teresa is only ten, but she's got thousands of followers. Sometimes people recognise her in the street. Mum got a second call when Britt used a bad swear word for an eight year old – the worst word.

Mum calls it a hat-trick when she gets calls about all three of us in the same week. Last time she said she kept expecting the phone to ring about the baby and make it a full set.

Auntie Jackie thought that was hilarious and they started acting out a phone call about what a naughty baby Baye was. Auntie Jackie put on this posh teacher voice.

"Hello, Mrs Layton?" Auntie Jackie said.

"Yeah?" Mum answered. "What's wrong this time?"

"I'm afraid it's baby Baye, Mrs Layton," Auntie Jackie went on.

"She's not even at your school," Mum said. "She's only a baby."

"But I can tell how badly behaved she is from here and so I thought it was worth a phone call."

They both howled with laughter at this.

It always happens. When I'm trying to stay out of trouble, it just seems to come and find me. I'm heading over the yard after lunch and am just minding my own business. But Alyssa and her gang shove past me and nearly knock me over.

I half think about ignoring them. I can't really be bothered with more drama today. But then I hear Alyssa's snide voice say, "Don't touch her. She probably can't afford to wash."

I can't stop myself. No one speaks about me like that. It's like a switch has been pressed in my head and my body. I lose it. I shove her hard in the chest, her pathetic mates squealing as I do. As she falls backwards, I see Mrs Hukin coming towards us.

*

An hour later I'm sitting in Mrs Hukin's office with Mum and Auntie Jackie either side of me. I just want this to be over with. Baye is sitting in her pram playing with one of my old Barbies.

I know how this all goes. Mrs Hukin tells us all how violence is not tolerated at this school. Mum defends me and says what a horrible mare Alyssa is. Mrs Hukin tells Mum to watch her language but agrees that what Alyssa did was not OK.

Talk, talk, talk. Nothing changes. If Mum swears too much or storms out, then I might get suspended and stay at home for a few days. But everyone knows that suspension won't do much. The whole thing is pointless. I'm only in Year Seven and we've been here so many times already.

Then Mrs Hukin starts.

"I think we need to try something different this time, ladies."

"How about dealing with that little cow bag who keeps starting on my daughter?" Mum says.

"I will talk to Alyssa separately, Mrs Layton," says Mrs Hukin. "Let's focus on Lacey, shall we?"

"Lacey's a good girl," says Mum. "She's the brainiest one of the lot of us."

Mum has always called me a brain box. Just because I used to do well in tests at primary school. Baye squeals and throws the Barbie on the floor.

"Baye Layton, you will get yourself a detention!" Mum tells Baye, adding, "Sorry, miss."

Mum acts weird with Mrs Hukin. Like she's a child again. One minute she's cheeky and rude, and the next she's trying not to get into trouble.

Mrs Hukin carries on.

"Lacey seems to find lunch-times most difficult and so I have an idea that could help. We have a music tutor visiting the school. They work with students, using music as therapy."

"Our Lacey doesn't need therapy." Auntie Jackie spits this out as if even the word "therapy" is revolting.

Mrs Hukin just carries on, as cool as a cucumber. I'm always amazed by how calm she stays.

"In which case she can just play music and stay out of trouble each lunch-time. Therapy or not, this is a chance for Lacey to have somewhere to go, to be safe and stay away from the kids she struggles with."

"Oh God. What are they gonna get her playing this time?" Auntie Jackie says, snorting and nudging Mum. "Remember that chuffing recorder?"

"Shut up, Jackie," Mum whispers. "I'd like to hear *you* try to play something." Then she looks at Mrs Hukin as if she's not sure. "They better not send Lacey home with some horrible-sounding thing. I'm not having a trumpet or anything like that in the house."

"If Lacey doesn't take up this offer, Mrs Layton," Mrs Hukin says, "I think we may need to look at other options for her schooling."

I see panic in Mum's eyes. I know the look – she'll either get angry and storm out swearing or turn into a little girl.

"She can't go anywhere else, miss," Mum replies, choosing the little girl. "Mountview is too far. I haven't got a car any more since Phil left."

Mrs Hukin smiles. She knows she's won.

"In that case, let's see what music can do, shall we? We might all be surprised."

CHAPTER 2

The next day I'm walking down the music corridor and can hear sounds coming from behind every door. There's the low *umpa pa* of some big blowy thing behind one door and then the loud smashing of a cymbal behind another. I've never been here at lunch-time. It almost sounds alive with all the different noises.

I'm meeting Mr Day in music room seven. It's down the end of the corridor. I keep walking, listening to the sounds. Angry guitars are followed by something light and airy and playful. Maybe a flute.

Music lessons are pretty much a total doss class, unless you can actually play an instrument. I just mess about on my phone while holding a bongo. The teacher only speaks to the kids who are interested anyway, which is fine by me.

That's why I'm not really bothered about coming here every day. I'll just do the same. Sit on my phone and pretend to play a bongo or something. Mr Day will try to get me to talk about my family and my feelings – they always do. I've had so many people trying to figure out why I'm like I am.

Back in Year Six, some woman with frizzy hair used to take me to a room full of dolls and ask me to act things out. I used to make stuff up. Get the dolls to start dog fights and then set them on each other and argue and light fire to themselves. The woman thought she was a genius. Like she'd uncovered all of my inner demons. Then I told her that it was all from some film I'd watched in bed.

As if I would ever act anything real out. There is no way I would have little dolly Mum and Dad shouting and swearing at each other and all us dolly kids crying upstairs. Dolly Daddy slamming the door and not coming back, while frizzy hair sits there smugly waiting for me to cry – I don't think so. Anyway, today I'll just hit my bongo if Mr Day asks me anything about my life or my feelings.

It's quiet behind the door of music room seven. I pause for a second before I open it. The silent door alongside all the loud ones somehow makes it feel important or something. When I push it open, I see a room full of instruments and a man sitting with some long boingy strings and a guitar. He looks up and smiles.

"Lacey?" he asks.

I nod and he gestures to come in. "Pop your stuff down and take a seat," he says. "I'll just finish this and then show you round."

Show me round? It's a music room not a mansion. I almost say this out loud but manage to keep it in. I dump my bag on the floor and then flop down into a chair on the other side of the room. I pretend that I'm not watching him and take my phone out of my bag.

"No phones in here," Mr Day says. He's going to be annoying, I can tell. I ignore him and look at my phone.

My home screen is a picture of me and all my sisters with dummies in our mouths doing peace signs with our fingers. Apart from Britt – she has her fingers the other way round. She's the naughtiest of all of us, way worse than me. I look at the picture and smile. We all still suck dummies. Mum gets really annoyed because we go in Baye's cot and steal them.

Mr Day's voice pipes up again, "There's zero reception in here anyway. Pop it on the desk and then come and help me with this."

The options start running around my head.
Do I ignore him, just do it or say something
back? I always have something to say. It
doesn't matter what a teacher says to me, my
brain can instantly come up with a million
cheeky responses. It's like a talent, but a talent
that only gets me into trouble. In this case the
top three options are:

1. *"I'm not putting my phone on your desk,
    sir. I don't even know you. You might
    have diseases."*

2. *"Don't worry about me, I don't need reception, sir. I'll just take some selfies. Careful, you might end up on my sister's Insta. She's got 24,000 followers."*

3. *"Why do you need my help? Are you thick, sir?"*

Some days I just give in and say the first thing that comes into my head. I get sent to ISO for the whole day then. Other days just one or two comments sneak out because they are too good to ignore. The idea of saying them makes me laugh inside and I just have to see how they sound on the outside.

Some days, but not very often, I try to be good and ignore the comments that pop up. That's when the teachers tell me I've had a good day. But it doesn't feel good to me. It feels boring and like I'm not being myself – like I'm pushing down the one thing I'm really good at.

I know it's not good to be skilful at being cheeky, but I bet everyone couldn't do it as well as me. A few times I've made teachers smile before they kick me out. Once, I told Mrs Freye she looked like a turkey twizzler and she hooted with laughter just before she sent me to ISO.

I look at Mr Day messing with all his wiry strings. I don't know why but I decide to push the comments down for now. I put my phone back in my bag and go over.

"Have you tuned a guitar before, Lacey?" Mr Day asks.

"I'm tone-deaf, sir," I say. "You should hear me on the karaoke."

"I would very much like to hear you on the karaoke." Then he passes me a little black plastic box that has a tiny screen on it and a clip on the back. "Sing a note and look at the screen."

"Are you actually joking, sir?" I say. "As if."

"OK, I will." Mr Day starts singing a note before I can say one of the million options that flood my brain. He gestures to the little screen. I go bright red on his behalf and look at the screen. Then he stops – thank God.

"What did it say?" he asks.

"G and a dash, sir," I say. "Sir, that was one of the most embarrassing things a teacher has ever done."

"Oh dear, I think if you found that embarrassing, things are going to get far worse, Lacey." Mr Day smiles to himself as if he is proud of being embarrassing. "You don't need to even sing. Just say a word slowly and it will tell you which note you are speaking in."

"I'm all right, sir, thanks," I say.

He laughs and looks back to the guitar.

"If you keep plucking this string here, I'll turn the tuning peg and you can tell me when the tuner says E." He passes me the guitar and then waits for me to start plucking.

"I'll probably break your guitar, sir."

"It was already broken," Mr Day says, "so you can't make it any worse." Then he just waits.

I can't think of a good reason not to, so I start plucking the string and he twists the peg and the noise changes. I look at the letters on the screen and when it says E, I stop plucking.

"Perfect. Now let's do the next string."

"This is a bit dull, sir," I say. "I thought you were meant to be finding out what's wrong with me."

"Well, feel free to tell me if there's something wrong, Lacey, or we can keep tuning the guitar. Totally up to you."

"You're weird, sir."

He smiles at this and then points to the next string.

"Next you're looking for an A," he says.

I start plucking. This is going to be a very long lunch break.

CHAPTER 3

The next day, I walk into the music room and Mr Day's sitting at the piano.

"I'm not tuning a piano, sir, if that's what you're thinking," I say.

"No, Lacey," he says, smiling. "We'll leave that to the professionals, shall we? You ever played a piano?"

"All the time, sir. Me and my whole family are always at piano recitals. We can't get enough."

"You're very funny, Lacey," Mr Day says.

"You're very funny, sir," I say. I pull a face that shows I mean a different kind of "funny".

"Take a seat and have a play."

"I'm not playing that thing," I tell him. "I told you I'm tone-deaf. Anyway, I'll probably break it."

Then Mr Day starts bashing away at the keys and making a horrible sound. I cover my ears and laugh.

"Sir, that's the worst sound I've ever heard."

"Exactly. You can't be worse than that."
Then Mr Day waits, just like he did with the
guitar plucking. If I play the thing it feels like
he's won, but I don't want to sit in silence for the
whole of lunch break.

Anyway, I don't mind him. Mr Day isn't
really like other teachers – he dresses normal
and has an accent like mine. He's not in a rush
and he thinks I'm funny. I don't know if he
would ever send me to ISO.

Just as I think that, all of the things I could
do to get Mr Day to send me out start popping
into my brain.

Smash a guitar up.

Call Mr Day the worst swear word.

Say stuff about his family.

Pour my water all over the piano.

The thoughts keep flooding in, but then I realise that I don't need to do any of them. Maybe it's because he's not staring at me, waiting angrily for me to do what he wants. Or maybe it's because there is silence in the room and I can hear all the thoughts clearly. There is another thought there too.

I could just turn around and walk out.
I don't actually have to be here.

I think about it in the silence. He's just looking at some piano music. I'm not sure that Mr Day would even tell Mrs Hukin if I did leave. He would probably just carry on messing around with the instruments all lunch-time.

The feeling of knowing that I can leave is enough. I have that power. I don't need to smash anything up, not today.

I sit down at the piano and press a white key. It makes a shy kind of sound as if it knows that I have no idea what I'm doing.

"Lovely, that's a D," Mr Day says. "You can try some more."

As I press more keys, Mr Day gets a pen out. After I have pressed them, he writes the note on the key.

"You'll get in right trouble for drawing on a school piano, sir," I say. "I would anyway."

"Here you go." Mr Day passes me the pen. "How about you write G on that one and then we are in it together? If I go down, you go down."

"I'm all right, sir – you can do it."

"Very sensible, Lacey," he says. "Anyway, it wipes off, so I think I'll be safe from detention."

"It sounds rubbish though, sir. How do people even make it sound good?"

"Well, there are certain notes that sound nice together," Mr Day explains. "It's just learning where they all are and which one to play next. Someone once said, 'There is no such thing as a wrong note.' It's what you play next that makes it better or worse. A bit like life, I think."

Then he starts drawing little dots and shapes onto some of the keys. As I'm watching him, I think about what he's just said.

"But that's not like life, sir," I say.

"In what way?"

"There are totally wrong notes in life and it doesn't matter what you do afterwards – it doesn't change the wrong thing from being wrong."

"Like what?" Mr Day asks.

I start thinking of so many wrong things. Things that I've done, that my sisters have done, and Mum, Auntie Jackie, Dad. Things which were so wrong that nothing would change them, no matter what anyone did next. Whichever note they played. It's making my head hurt thinking about it.

"I know what you're doing, sir," I say. "I'm not thick."

"I realised that you were far from thick the moment I met you, Lacey," Mr Day says. "Shall we keep playing? Look, if you're worried about it sounding 'right', then try this. Just play the black notes."

I'm relieved to be taken away from the thoughts of wrong things. I place my hands on the black keys and start pressing.

The sound is different. The notes work. I smile to myself and keep on playing. The whole room is full of sounds that feel right. When I finally stop, the silence feels loud. I wait for thoughts to roll into my mind of what funny thing I can say, or of what I did wrong, but they don't come. It's like my mind is empty for a moment.

"How did that feel?" Mr Day asks as he goes back to drawing things on the keys.

"Yeah, good, sir," I mumble. Then I add, "If the black notes sound like that, why do people bother with the white ones?"

"Well, if you use all of the notes, you can make even more beautiful music. There's more chance for it not to work, but there is a greater chance of making something incredible and unique. It's like if you only used the bit of your brain that already knew things and didn't try to learn anything else in case you got it wrong. It would be a waste of brain."

"Miss Hukin says that I'm wasting my brain," I say.

"Do you think she's right?" Mr Day asks.

I shrug. "I think family's more important, and having a laugh, than knowing about algebra."

"Can't you do all of those things – have a laugh, love your family AND learn about algebra?" he says.

"You try having a laugh in a Maths lesson, sir!"

"Mmm, good point. Do you want to try a saxophone?" Mr Day says, pointing to a shiny instrument in the corner.

*

For the next few days, we tune and play different instruments, hit drums with sticks and make some horrible noises on flutes and trombones. Every day, my eyes flick back to the piano. I want to play those black notes again. To make the sounds that work. The sounds that cleared my head of all the thoughts.

On Friday at the end of lunch, Mr Day packs up the instruments and says, "Thank you for a lovely week, Lacey. I've really enjoyed it."

"Did I say that you're weird, sir?" I ask.

"You did, thank you. Let me know if there is an instrument that you particularly enjoyed this week and want to focus on. Otherwise we can just keep trying things out."

The words spill out before I can even try and be cool and pretend I don't care.

"I want to play the piano, sir."

CHAPTER 4

"Are you cured, Lacey?" Auntie Jackie says on Saturday morning. "Has music saved your poor unfortunate soul?"

"Yeah, course it has," I say, smiling. I'm making up the baby's bottle with some milky tea.

"I hope you're not telling him how horrible we all are?" Auntie Jackie says. She's standing at the door and sucking in on her cigarette, peering over at me suspiciously.

"Course I am, Jackie," I say. "All I do is sit there crying at a piano telling Mr Day how my auntie Jackie is ruining my life."

"You better not mention my name to some goody-two-shoes therapist, that's all I'm saying. I don't want my name turning up in some report."

Mum looks over at me as I put the bottle into Baye's outstretched arms.

"She knows not to say anything, don't you, girl?" Mum says.

I just nod. Mum always tells us never to say anything to anyone official. She says that everything that happens in this house is private and can be dealt with privately. "We don't need teachers or coppers or the social getting involved in our business."

It makes me wonder why someone would be interested in our business in the first place. I

don't think anyone would be bothered even if
I did tell them everything that goes on. Not that
I'm going to.

"What's he got you playing anyway?" Mum
says.

"Just different stuff," I reply. "Piano, flute,
guitar, all sorts."

Mum smiles at me. "I think it's good, me.
You're lucky, Lacey. I wish I'd had a chance like
that. I always wanted to play a flute. I think
they sound lovely, I do." Mum looks sad for a
second and then Jackie's voice pipes up.

"As if. You wouldn't be able to play a
tambourine in tune!"

Mum sticks her fingers up at Jackie and they
both laugh.

It's Baye's birthday today. She's two. Mum
got her present from some shop where you don't

have to pay for things straight away. She'd promised she wouldn't go there again because last time she couldn't pay it off in time and got into trouble. But Mum said it was the only way to get her little princess a birthday present.

It's a huge plastic fairy castle with pink turrets and loads of tiny windows. I think Baye would rather have a cheap football from the One Stop, but I didn't say anything. Everyone is coming over later for a party. I'm going to look after Baye all day, make sure that she's OK.

*

When people arrive, they're all carrying presents. Baye totters over to see what she's got. The Turners from down the road have brought her a massive bar of chocolate. Uncle Scott and Auntie Rach give her a huge box wrapped up in silver paper. (They're not really our auntie and uncle, but they've known us so long they might as well be.)

"It's not new, but it's never been used," Rach says. "Our Chelsea wasn't interested."

Baye tears off the wrapping. There is a purple plastic keyboard inside with buttons shaped like stars and moons, and sliders to change the sounds. As I look at the keys, I think about the piano in music room seven. It makes me want to play it.

When Baye's stopped pressing all of the buttons, I bend down next to her and gently press some of the black keys. They are on a setting that makes them sound like cats meowing, so I change it to sound as much like

a real piano as possible. Then I whisper into Baye's ear, "Listen, just play the black notes."

I start pressing the keys. The room goes quieter and Baye's face lights up. For a moment it's magic, then she snatches the keyboard back. She starts hammering away at it and changes the setting back to cats. Then the sound of Auntie Jackie's voice calls out from the kitchen.

"Well, la di da, look at you, Miss Fancy Pants. You need to watch her – Lacey's had one week with that music man and she's already changing."

"Shut your face, Jackie," Mum says.

I smile back sarcastically, but I know Auntie Jackie means it. She is always scared of new things. She hates it when new people move onto the street, or when any of us get a new friend. It's like it somehow threatens her place in the family. I better not talk about the piano or the music lunch-times any more. She's watching me.

*

A couple of hours later, when everyone is arguing about some TV show, I see the familiar blue car pull up outside. A weird feeling of fear mixed with excitement rushes around my body. I know this is not going to be good, but I can't help the silly little girl part of me from thinking, *Daddy's home!*

Everyone knows it's time to leave when they see him. The kitchen empties, apart from Auntie Jackie and the rest of us. Baye rushes over and Dad scoops her up, flipping her upside down and blowing raspberries on her tummy.

"What the hell are you doing here?" Mum's voice is loud.

"It's my baby's birthday," Dad says. "I wouldn't miss it for the world."

It doesn't take long for Mum and Dad to start shouting. After Auntie Jackie has gone, they keep screaming at each other, so I scoop Baye up and whisper to the others to go to our room. We snuggle up on the bed and turn the telly up loud like we used to when Dad still lived here. We ignore the sounds coming up the stairs.

When the others are all asleep and everything's gone quiet, I sneak downstairs and peek into the kitchen. Dad's gone and Mum is sitting at the table with her head in her hands. She doesn't look great, but she's OK. I try to sneak back up, but she hears me.

"You OK, Lacey?" Mum asks.

I nod and she smiles sadly, tears streaking down her face.

"I'm so sorry, love," Mum says. "Are the girls OK?"

"We're fine, Mum," I say. "Get yourself to bed, eh?"

"I love you girls, you know that?"

"We love you too, Mum," I say.

At the bottom of the stairs Baye's new keyboard is lying on its side. I pick it up and take it back upstairs to safety.

CHAPTER 5

Over the next few weeks Mr Day tells me what all the dots and marks on the keys mean. There are different shapes and colours to show which notes go together. All the stars work with each other and the blue squares are a jazz scale with a funny name. I hear some of the notes that the white keys make together and they sound perfect. I add the things I learn to the black notes, and the sounds I make get better and better.

Mr Day just lets me play. He says he will teach me how to read music or play proper songs if I want. But I prefer just making stuff

up, so he sits with his eyes closed and listens.
He calls what I'm doing "composing", which
sounds pretty fancy to me.

One day when I finish playing, he opens his eyes and it looks like he might have been crying a bit.

"You all right, sir?" I ask. I'm used to his weirdness now.

"You have a natural gift on the piano, Lacey. It's incredible."

"Yeah, all right, sir, whatever you say." I laugh and pick up my bag. But as I look back at him wiping his eyes, I think he might be telling me the truth.

"Thanks, sir," I say. "See you tomorrow."

Some days I speed up my fingers and play the stars and the moons, and I can make music that sounds happy. When I finish, I can't stop smiling. Other days I play squares and dots that sound sad and make me feel strange and churned up. But even on those days, when I stop playing, all of the thoughts vanish for a while.

The more I play, the less I think about afterwards. It must be what people mean when they say they're calm or relaxed. I never knew that I wasn't calm or relaxed until now.

Sometimes I picture a scene and then find the notes to go along with it, like a soundtrack. The scene might be a nervous teacher taking a class, or kids getting into a fight in the playground, or Mum and Auntie Jackie in the kitchen. Mr Day loved the kitchen song, even though I didn't tell him that's what it was.

Today I'm making up a song that sounds strong and powerful. The notes are loud and long and make me feel bigger. When I finish, I close my eyes and enjoy the silence, not bothered that Mr Day is right there.

When I open my eyes, he smiles and says, "Do you think you would like to add lyrics to any of your pieces? Do any words come up for you when you play?"

"No, sir," I say. "All the words vanish – that's why I like it so much. My brain stops thinking of the next thing I need to say or do, and it forgets about all the things before."

"How wonderful," he says. Then we sit there in the silence not needing to say anything else.

At home I've been practising on Baye's keyboard every night. I take it in the bathroom, lock the door and then turn the volume down low so no one can hear. Playing on the plasticky keyboard doesn't feel quite as good, but I still like it.

Mr Day says that if I practise my scales, it will help me with my compositions. That's what he calls the songs that I make up. So that's what I do. Night after night in the steamy bathroom I practise my scales over and over again. Until someone comes banging on the door and tells me they are going to poo themselves unless I get out of there.

Today when I wake up, I hear a song, as if I have dreamed it. I can't wait to play it. I walk to school, past the new-build estate and then past the train station. All the while the song is playing over and over in my head.

In English I'm still thinking of the song when Mrs Yardley asks me what I think of the book we are reading. I lose the song and feel annoyed, so I can't help but say the first thing that pops up.

"It's rubbish, miss. What's the point in reading old-fart books that have nothing to do with what's really happening? I want to read about people like me, not about old posh people like you."

Everyone in the class sniggers and shuffles, knowing that it might all kick off. I've been a bit better recently. I've not felt the need to wind people up so much, but Mrs Yardley has annoyed me by making me lose my song.

"Lacey, I have to send you out for talking to me like that," she says. "But it's an interesting point. If you can't connect with a character, then how can you enjoy a story? I will save that discussion for when you are here tomorrow. Today we will continue our work on creating a call to action based on the text. Can you remember what a call to action is, Lacey?" Mrs Yardley asks as I'm clearing my desk.

"Save Lacey Layton! Sack the old farts!" I shout.

Everyone laughs hard at this. I look at Mrs Yardley's sad face and I feel a pang of guilt. She's actually not that bad, but I couldn't help it. She totally set me up for that one.

"Lacey, please go to isolation and think about how you could be a little kinder to people," she says.

*

In ISO, Mrs Hukin looks up from her desk and gives me a sad smile.

"I haven't seen so much of you lately, Lacey. I thought we'd maybe turned a corner. What happened?"

"I told Mrs Yardley that her book choice was boring and that she was a posh old fart," I say.

I can see Mrs Hukin hiding a smile.

"Mmm, I see. How about lunch-times? I saw Mr Day in the corridor the other day. He says you have a real talent for the piano?"

I shrug and twiddle with my bag strap.

"He is very concerned about what will happen when he leaves," Mrs Hukin says. "He wants you to keep playing."

I sit up straight, my eyes wide.

"What do you mean when he leaves?" I ask.

"We only have him till the end of term, then he goes to another school."

I freeze.

"So, we need to figure out what to do in two weeks," says Mrs Hukin. "How to keep you playing."

But I'm not listening to her any more. My eyes are stinging and my brain is full. The bell rings for lunch and I jump up and run all the way to music room seven. I open the door and see Mr Day and some oversized Year Eleven kid sitting at the drums. I slam the door hard, making them both look at me.

"What's the point in this?" I shout.

"Hi, Lacey, you're a bit early," Mr Day says.

"You're just going to leave," I say. "So what's been the point in any of this?" I feel tears prick up in my eyes and I wipe them away angrily.

Mr Day tells the Year Eleven to leave and then sits at his desk.

"Did you not know that the sessions were only until Easter, Lacey? I should have made that clearer. I'm sorry."

"It's a load of crap, sir. It's pointless – like the dolls."

"I'm moving, but the piano isn't, Lacey," says Mr Day. "I've been talking to Mrs Hukin to figure out how to keep you playing."

"I don't want to keep playing," I say. "You tricked me."

"How do you feel I tricked you, Lacey?"

"Stop saying my name. You don't know me. You know nothing about me. I should have known you would just leave. That you'd make out like I was good, that you liked me, and then just leave anyway."

"We still have two weeks," he says.

"I don't want them. I should never have come in the first place. Stupid piano." Then I smash my hand down on the keys. The sound is loud and jarring and pain shoots up my wrist. The silence that follows is filled by the slam of the door on my way out.

CHAPTER 6

I spend almost the whole of the next week in ISO. I don't even try to stop the comments from coming out when they pop into my brain. They are loud and constant and even the other kids seem shocked by how cheeky I am. At home I shove the plastic keyboard down into Baye's toy pile, covering it with teddies and princess costumes so that I can't see it.

Lunch-times are the worst. I roam around the playground picking fights and calling things out to people. Alyssa is not pleased that I'm back.

"I thought they had put her in some special-needs music class at lunch-time?" she calls loudly as I strut past her.

I swivel on my toes and face her.

"Say that again, Alyssa," I demand. "I dare you."

Alyssa can see on my face that something's different, that I'm worse than usual. Her face flushes and she looks at the ground.

"I didn't say anything," she says.

I smile, enjoying my power.

"I thought so," I reply.

Sometimes the song that I dreamed plays in my head. Instead of trying to hold on to it, I drown it out with jokes and banter. Crushing the life out of it.

*

On the last day before the Easter holidays I get handed a note from the teacher in form class.

Dear Lacey,

It's my last day at the school today.

I have missed our sessions the last couple of weeks. Partly because I think that the talent you have shown for composition and song-writing is truly something special. But also because I very much enjoyed your company. If you would like to come and play this lunch-time, then it would be great to be able to say goodbye.

From your "weird" music teacher,
Mr Day (Rob)

I screw the note up and throw it towards the bin. It misses.

"Lacey Layton, pick that up immediately, please," the teacher says. "Wouldn't it be nice if your last day of term wasn't spent in isolation?"

I can't help it. The options flood into my brain.

"Wouldn't it be nice, miss, if I didn't have to look at your miserable face for the last day?"

"Out."

In ISO, Mrs Hukin comes over to my desk and sits next to me. She looks tired. Her hair looks sad and her shoulders are tight and slumped at the same time. I start to form these observations into a sentence that could easily get me suspended, but she interrupts my thoughts.

"So, Lacey, I have some good news," Mrs Hukin says.

"You've found a new hairdresser?" I joke.

"Very funny. No, I have found you a piano ... well, a keyboard."

Even the sound of the word shakes me up.

"What are you on about, miss?" I ask.

"Well, you might have been wandering about getting into trouble for the last two weeks, but meanwhile we have been trying to think of a way to help you."

"I don't need help. I'm fine," I say.

"Of course you are, Lacey, but Mr Day wanted to find a way to keep you playing. We know that the chances of you going to the music rooms at lunch-times when he leaves are very slim. We have an electric piano and the caretaker has said he can deliver it."

"Deliver it where?"

"To your house, Lacey," says Mrs Hukin. "If you can find the space for it, then we would like to offer you a piano."

I can't help but howl with laughter. It's the smug pleased look on her face and the effort she must have gone to, all for this grand gesture.

"Miss, you're on another planet," I say.

"We think it's important that you keep playing, Lacey."

"It's never going to happen. The idea of a piano in my house is ridiculous, even if we had space, miss. My sisters would trash it."

"It's a keyboard, not a full-sized piano," says Mrs Hukin. "Could it go in your bedroom? Then you could practise every day away from the rest of the family."

"I share my bedroom with two sisters, miss. There is stuff piled high against every single wall. I have to share a bed with Teresa. Do you want to suggest to my mum that we try to 'squeeze in a piano' – sorry 'keyboard' – as well?"

"Oh well, maybe we can find a way."

"I don't want to play the thing any more anyway," I say.

*

At lunch-time I find myself slowly walking down the music corridor, listening in to the sounds behind the doors. There are strong, confident drums behind number one. A flitting violin behind another.

When I get to music room seven, I hear it. The sound of the piano coming through the door. I slowly open it a crack and peer in. Mr Day is sitting with his back to me playing a beautiful song. I've never heard him play before, not like this. I assumed he couldn't really play after he smashed his hands down on the keys and made the hideous sound.

I can tell from Mr Day's back that he is breathing with the music. That he's feeling the way I do when I play. Calm and empty.

I close my eyes and try to tune in to that feeling, allowing the sound to take me away. When the song ends, he turns around before I can hide. So I stare back at him. Our eyes lock and I can feel my throat tighten up. But it gets

too much. When I can't bear it any more, I say,
"Bye, sir ... Thanks." And I turn and run back
down the corridor.

CHAPTER 7

The first day of the Easter holidays I'm in a terrible mood. My sisters are all being loud and annoying. They're screaming and slapping each other with a tortilla wrap, while Teresa films it. I try to hide, but I feel like I can't get away from them and their noise.

Sometimes I feel like an outsider in my own family. I don't think the others question anything, but I do. I question if it's OK to swear and shout and take the mickey out of school as if learning anything new is a bad thing. I question if it's OK to tell us to start fights with other kids because their mum might have said something horrible about Auntie Jackie. I question whether it will be like this for ever.

I question it all but then I feel instantly guilty. I know Mum and Auntie Jackie love us more than anything. Mum works so hard to look after us. And so I choose to accept it. It's the accepting it that's putting me in a bad mood today.

I don't know why I feel so angry. Tomorrow I will forget about it and be back to normal. Just go along with everything – slap someone with a tortilla wrap, howl with laughter and feel the safety of being "one of the Layton girls". It does feel safe. I know they would all do anything for me – literally anything.

I go outside and walk, ignoring the calls from the kids on the rec. I don't know where I'm going, but I walk down past the new-build estate and look in at the neat bins and the short green grass.

As I keep walking, the song from my dreams plays in my head, as if it's grateful for the space and silence. I don't smother it this time. I let the song play and imagine the keys of the piano playing.

As I walk past the train station, the notes in my head merge with others and it sounds strange and jarring. I'm not sure what's

happening for a minute. It's only when I shush
my song that I realise there's real music playing
somewhere. The sound of a piano coming from
inside the station.

It's a soft playful song that jumps around.
I follow the sounds until I'm standing inside the
station, looking at a toothless old guy playing
the piano.

I never come to the train station. Mum says trains are a rip-off, so we always get the bus. I never knew there was a piano in here.

After a while, I perch on a low wall outside a shop with the shutters down. I settle in, as if I've come to my very own concert. The toothless man smiles at me and continues playing as people bustle past on their way to or from the trains.

He looks around and plays songs for everyone. Loud, dramatic booming pieces for the businessmen who are late, and then quiet tentative pieces for the people who are lost. It's like watching a music video – the different songs make the stories of the people shine out.

Most people ignore the music, a couple glancing and smiling as they pass. Then suddenly the man stops and picks up his bags and leaves. As he walks past me, he pretends to lift an imaginary hat, winks and then he says, "Your turn."

I go red and smile shyly. I can't play a piano in the middle of a train station. Not with all these people around. As I'm thinking about it, another pianist sits and plays. This time it's a young woman with braided hair and a bright blue skirt.

After her a man in a suit plays classical, then an old lady comes along whose husband watches her play proudly. A couple of kids run up and bash the keys. I really want to tell them to play the black notes only so they can feel what playing the right notes feels like.

I sit there for the whole day until my bum goes numb and my belly rumbles. I sit there until it starts going darker outside and there are fewer and fewer people getting off the trains. I sit there until the station is empty and it's just me and the piano. Then I realise that I have been waiting to play my song. That I was never going to go home until I'd played it.

CHAPTER 8

"Where the hell have you been?" Mum says as I walk into the kitchen.

I haven't really thought of what I'm going to say. My brain starts filling with all of the things that I definitely can't say.

"Well, Mother, I have been figuring out a composition on the piano."

"Actually, Mother, I felt suffocated in this house with you lot. So I went to figure out who I actually want to be and what I want to do with my life."

"I had a dream about music, Mummy, and the song has been calling me until I found somewhere to play it. I'm terribly, terribly sorry."

I laugh out loud as that last thought pops into my brain.

"It's not funny, Lacey," Mum says. "You could have been dead for all I knew. It's nearly midnight."

"Well, I'm not," I say. "I'm here, fully alive and back where I belong. Stuck with you lot."

"Very funny. Get to bed and tell your sisters to go to sleep, will you? I can hear them shrieking. If I catch you sneaking out again, Lacey Layton, you will be in big trouble, you hear me?"

*

For the next week I sneak out of the back door every night and go to the piano at the station.

It takes me ages to finish figuring out the song in my head, but when I do it sounds amazing. One of the security guards and the nice woman from the sandwich shop clap when

I finish playing the whole thing for the first time. I go red, but it makes me feel so happy inside.

I don't ever want to come and play in the day in front of hundreds of people, but I don't mind the cleaners and the security guards and the shopkeepers closing their shutters and listening.

Tonight I don't want to stop and so I play through the night. I only realise that it's nearly morning when people in suits start arriving for their trains. The toothless man appears next to me.

"You can really play, lady," he says. Then he smiles sadly. "They are taking this piano next week."

"Taking it where?" I ask.

"I don't know, but it's going."

"But it's the only place I can play," I say.

"Me too, kid."

Then I stand up and let him sit. The toothless man starts playing a sad song. As I turn to leave, he calls out over the music, "If you want to save the piano, then come and play tomorrow at midday. The news people are coming with their cameras."

"I can't play in front of people."

He nods as if he understands and carries on with his song.

I turn and run. Back past the new-build estate and then I sneak up past the rec, avoiding the windows of any spying eyes.

I silently open the back door, but instantly see the light coming from the kitchen and I know I'm caught.

"Lacey Layton, where the HELL have you been?" yells Mum. "Get in here now!"

When I walk in, Mum's in her dressing gown and Auntie Jackie's round in hers. Mum must have called her when she realised I wasn't in bed.

"Your sisters have said you've been out every night," Mum says. "Sneaking into bed at all hours."

I will kill them, I think. But first of all I need to come up with some reason for Mum. Something believable but better than the truth.

"Where have you been going?" Mum asks.

The options fly around my head. Then the truth pops up and all of a sudden it doesn't sound so bad.

So I bite my lip, lower my head with embarrassment and just say it, "I've been playing the piano at the train station."

"You what?" It's Auntie Jackie's voice, quiet and dangerous.

"I've been making songs up and there's a piano at the station, so I go there to practise."

Mum seems confused, but Auntie Jackie looks furious. Then they look at each other and their expressions change and their faces crack up. They howl with laughter.

I sigh. They keep laughing until they are holding their sides and wiping their eyes. Eventually, Mum calms down enough to say, "Sneaking out all night to play the ruddy piano?"

Auntie Jackie says, "You're an embarrassment, Lacey."

"That's why I go at night," I say. "No one's even there." Then I add quietly, "Mr Day thought I shouldn't give up. He thought I was pretty good."

Mum smiles sadly, but Auntie Jackie doesn't care.

"Mr sodding Day's been putting all sorts in your head." Then Auntie Jackie looks at Mum, waiting for her to agree. "She shouldn't be going to the station on her own."

For a second I think Mum might take my side. But then she seems to shake off whatever she was thinking and snaps, "You'll have to practise at school. Train stations are rough. I don't want you going there again. Do you hear me?"

"Not as rough as this house!" I shout back. "I hate you and I hate this place." The anger I'm feeling could get me into real trouble, I know it.

"Get up those stairs before I get hold of you, young lady," Mum says.

I run out of the kitchen and up the stairs, panic and rage flooding my body.

I lock myself in the bathroom, look at myself in the mirror and breathe. It's over. The piano is going anyway, so I suppose it doesn't matter.

I think of all the people I saw playing on the day that I found it. They didn't all look posh and fancy. There must be loads of people like me and the toothless man who don't have pianos and can only play at the station. Who don't have the money or the space or the right life to play anywhere else.

All of a sudden it feels important to try to save it. Not for me. After this, I won't ever go and play it again. I will stay away and go back to being a normal Layton girl. But I need to do this for other people.

People who need to feel the feeling of playing the right notes. So maybe I just need to go and play my song one more time, for me and for them. Tomorrow at midday.

CHAPTER 9

I know the best way to get out of the house without Mum getting suspicious. At 11.45, when she gets in from work, I slope into the kitchen.

"I'm bored," I moan. Mum hates it when any of us say this. She always says the same thing – "Only boring people get bored. Go out and find something to do. Just don't make it too exciting, whatever you do. I don't want the police knocking on my door."

I don't make it too easy, too obvious.

"But it's raining," I pretend to complain.

"Out!"

I smile to myself and stroll out of the door.

I feel sick with nerves. I'm nervous about going to the piano during the daytime. About playing it in front of people. I'm nervous about a TV crew pointing cameras at me and asking questions. But also I'm excited. It feels right. Like for once in my life I'm playing the right notes and making the right choices. I walk out and head to the station.

When I get there, it's quieter than I thought. There is just the toothless man, another homeless woman, a cameraman looking bored and a lady with smooth hair and a green suit holding a microphone.

This isn't going to save the piano. This is an advert to get rid of the thing.

I go over to the toothless man.

"What's happening?" I ask.

"No one's turned up," he says. "Well, except for you."

"Don't people care?"

"Not enough, kid. Let's have one final play, shall we?"

He sits down at the piano and I hear the lady with smooth hair start speaking.

"We are live at Central Station, saying goodbye to the piano that has stood on its concourse for three years. The council have said they can no longer afford to maintain it. Regular players have arrived to play their last song."

The toothless man starts playing an upbeat song which somehow still manages to sound tragic. This can't be how it ends. There must be people who care, people who are fierce and loyal and will do something.

I try to think of what I can do, who I can ask for help. Then it comes to me. Who is fierce, who will fight for me and do anything it takes? I take out my phone and make the call. Then I go and borrow a Sharpie and a piece of cardboard from the sandwich shop.

Five minutes later Teresa arrives.

"Did you tell Mum where you were going?" I ask her.

"No," Teresa says. "What's up?"

"I need you to put this on your Insta live. Tell people to come and save the piano. They are taking it away for no reason. People need it."

"I'm not putting some weird old man on my Insta."

"Not him," I say. "Me."

Teresa looks at me like I have lost my mind.

"I'm playing next."

"You're tone-deaf, Lacey," Teresa says.

"Just watch and film it, OK?" I say.

"Well, it's not my usual content, but OK. People love a sob story and music goes down well on lives. I might get some new followers."

By the time the toothless man finishes his last song, a few more people have gathered around, interested by the camera. I sit at the piano, my head buzzing and hands shaking. I look at Teresa, who is pointing her phone at me. I hold up the cardboard sign and lean it against the stool.

SAVE OUR PIANO!
COME TO THE STATION NOW!

The lady in the green suit talks into the microphone again.

"Welcome back to the station, where we have a young player who is sending a clear message to the council. Is it too little too late?"

I place my hands on the keys and breathe in. My mind clears and my hands stop shaking. I start playing my piece and the rest of the world seems to breathe in around me.

As I send the notes out into the universe, I relax and enjoy what might be my last time playing the song. I can hear movement around me but I keep my eyes on the piano, adding trills and silences that have not been there before. I'm playing in a way that I haven't played before. Maybe because now I know people are listening.

As I'm coming to the end, I hear loud footsteps running down the shiny station floor. I play the last note, let it ring out and enjoy the

emptiness of my brain for a second. Only then
do I look up to see who has arrived.

My heart wobbles as I turn to see Mum,
Auntie Jackie and Britt all staring at me.
They're breathing hard as if they ran the
whole way. Baye is sucking a dummy in her
pram. I smile apologetically. The last thing
I want is everything to kick off live on telly.

Behind them, loads of people from school and other kids who live round ours start arriving. They all follow Teresa on Insta, so they must have seen it. Some of their parents walk up behind them to see what's happening, craning their necks at the camera and the presenter, trying to figure out what's going on.

SAVE OUR PIANO!
COME TO THE STATION NOW!

Slowly more people gather – some people I know and some people I've never seen before. There are passers-by pulling suitcases or pushing prams, people looking up from their phones or taking their headphones off. They're all stopping and waiting for me to play.

I look back to Mum and Auntie Jackie and then play a few notes from the kitchen song.

"Lacey Layton …" It's Auntie Jackie's cold voice.

Mum puts her hand up and stops her.

"Shut it, Jackie, for once, will you?" Mum says. "I want to hear her."

Jackie looks furious but does what she's told. I keep playing as more and more people arrive. I can hear the TV woman in the background talking to her audience, telling them what's happening.

As I finish the song, I look back up at Mum. Her face scrunches up and she wipes her eyes angrily as if she's cross for feeling anything.

"I'm sorry, Mum," I say. "I won't come again."

"What the hell are you talking about, Lacey?" I'm not sure what Mum's thinking or feeling – if she is angry or sad or embarrassed. "I had no idea you could do that. No idea. I thought you were tone-deaf. I thought you'd been playing ruddy 'Chopsticks' not ruddy Chopin."

"Do you even know who Chopin is, Mum?" I ask.

"No, but that's not the point. Lacey, you're incredible and you can come and play whenever you want."

"I can't, Mum. That's the point. They're getting rid of the piano."

I realise quickly that this is going to get messy. Mum's face changes and she looks around, deciding who to blame.

Mum goes straight up to the woman with smooth hair and snatches the microphone from her hands. She looks right into the camera as she speaks.

"I've never heard my baby play the piano before today. If you lot from the sodding station or the council or wherever take it away from her, I swear to God I will come down there myself and there'll be hell to pay. Won't there, girls?!" Mum calls out.

Teresa and Britt push Baye over to the camera and start shouting, "Save our piano."

Everyone in the station cheers and claps and starts dancing around in front of the camera, shouting, "Save our piano! Save our piano! Save our piano!" as if they are at a football match.

I laugh and Teresa shows me her Insta.
The likes and comments are ticking up into the
thousands.

"We're going viral," she says.

I smile to myself, feeling sure now that the piano will be saved. As I look around at the crowd, I see Mr Day smiling over at me. He waves and puts his thumbs up. I wave back, my eyes suddenly filling with tears.

I know that the piano will be safe, but also I know that I'm safe too. I don't need to choose between who I want to be and who I am. I can be both. I can use all of my notes. I can be cheeky and funny and get into trouble, but I can work hard too. I can play the piano and use all of my brain and still be a Layton girl.

Our books are tested
for children and young people by
children and young people.

Thanks to everyone who consulted on
a manuscript for their time and effort in
helping us to make our books better
for our readers.